I0624561

We Can't Let You In

—A Diary from the PyreDees Plague of 2016—

A Young Adult Novella
By Sandy Lender

Dragon Hoard Press
An imprint of IYF Publishing

Dragon Hoard Press is an imprint of IYF Publishing.
We Can't Let You In
—A Diary from the PyreDees Plague of 2016—

ISBN-10: 0-99987801-8
ISBN: 978-099987801-9

Dragon Hoard Press
Beverly Hills, FL

First Edition: 2018

Day One of Writing This By Hand
September 26th

I can't even. Mom handed me a pen and a spiral notebook, and told me to "do it old school." Considering we're 99% positive civilization has collapsed, I'm going Ye Olde World at this point.

She also used one of her TV phrases that she likes: "Your host will enjoy the tactile sensation."

I swear she's a bigger nerd than I am. I told her the *Stargate-SG1* references don't work on me because I wasn't alive for most of that series. I mean, it DID end in, what? 2006? 2007? She says I was watching it from the womb. Whatever. Then she told me to be our historian.

That got deep really fast.

I get that only the survivors write the history books, but the world's in big trouble if I'm the one documenting our actions for the future. Because I don't have a lot of faith in us humans at this point.

I'm not implying we're all immoral—like Nurse Parsons suggests all.the.time.—or that we're all stupid—like Tech Stevens flat out tells us to our faces. I just think we—as in the people who blindly trust our governments of the world—have gone complacent.

> Complacent: not caring enough to look up the real
> definition to write it out all the way.

How's that for chronicling history? There's gonna be a scrapbook from my BF, my history textbook from Mrs. Johnson's World Civ 3rd Period, and this green spiral notebook of whacky "What Chloe Thinks of The World" notes for some archeologist to find 1,000 years from now.

To be serious—which is difficult when I'm trying NOT to consider whether my M.I.A. bestie is alive or in danger or something worse—I want to say that history right now is difficult to think about. History is currently not my fave subject, even though that's the book my hand reached out and grabbed when we left the house. History and medicine. Both officially suck as far as I'm concerned right now.

I'd rather lose myself in the Bronte book Mom's always quoting and has—of course—in her office. You know, she has a bona fide second edition copy of *Jane Eyre* that she bought at Haworth's actual gift shop? It's in two volumes, because that's how big books were published back then (hold on—back then being 1847—and we're coming up on the anniversary!), and both volumes are in this fancy shadow box with a needlepoint thing Mom made back when she had time to make crafty stuff. Anyway, if we all die here because our government sprayed us with noxious chemicals, and some archeologist or alien from another world finds this notebook (and translates it) and then you find a broken-down-pile-of-rubble house in Collier County with a fancy shadow box containing the antiquarian version of *Jane Eyre*—yeah—you've put that puzzle together.

Gawd. Bill is trying to get everyone to meet in the conference room so we can discuss water rationing. Because that hasn't been discussed enough. Mom has already said that when the rain stops, the air should be clear of the spray and we can get the gallons of water out of the trunk of our car. We had to leave those when we ran in last week ahead of the spray. So there's more water coming. He needs to chillax. I'll write more tomorrow.

Day Two of Doing It Old School
September 27th

Mom had the nerve to ask me if I'm using complete sentences. Complete sentences. When the world is basically gone, the actual Internet is down, and the last radio report Mike the Janitor could get said 50 percent of Europe was dead and 75 percent of South and Central America, she's worried about my grammar.

Yes, believe it or not, I'm alone in my age bracket in a life plan community for the elderly in the retirement capital of the universe—also known as Southwest Florida—writing complete sentences by hand in a paper notebook. Why? Because I'm the nerd who was, until last week, an "A" student at Gulf Coast High who had just received her learner's permit early because of an excellent record.

I was the nerd with zero prospects for a date to the homecoming dance after the homecoming game. In fact, I'm so far out of the running for a date that I'm not sure which night is the game and which night the dance.

Think about that. If you have the dance on Friday night, the self-absorbed girls don't have time to get their hair and makeup and nails done at a salon after school. But if you have the dance on Saturday night to accommodate the fancy girls, you run the risk of a really downer mood if The Sharks lose the game the night before. Or does anyone care 24 hours later?

Shell and I had considered we might dress up and go—separately, yet together—so we could at least see it. But then we thought people would start rumors about us because people have nothing better to do except worry about other people's sexual orientations in this society. Don't get me wrong—I don't care if someone is a lesbian. But I'm not basing my friendship choices on who you want to get with.

Make a note of that, Archeologists of the Future. In 2016, all we humans care about is who other people want to sleep with. And forming cliques.

I thought the collapse of civilization might be some kind of great equalizer as far as that nerd versus cool kids goes. Not correct. I see the staff at the center in their little cliques just like high school, just like the old world. Why bother? All it takes is one mosquito getting in here and we're all melting from the inside in the same way.

Now that's a great equalizer: melting from the inside out.

I exaggerated that a bit. Is it too early in "Chloe's Diary o' Death" to explain the mosquito crap? They really got a bad rap in all this. They were just doing what mosquitoes do. Drinking blood to survive. Team Edward and all.

Then the CDC got heavily involved.

I wish the CDC had done it differently. I feel for the poor women whose babies were affected by Zika virus. I'm not heartless. I'd like to have a baby someday and I want my baby to be healthy.

It's shocking to consider thousands—literally thousands—of babies were being born with birth defects in Puerto Rico and across Latin America. It's gut-wrenching to imagine a new mom holding her little baby, kissing his tiny sweet face, her tears falling on his skin as she has to worry for how he may or may not develop. All because a virus got into her blood. This is the year 2016. How can we not stop a simple virus that makes some people have a headache for a week from doing so much harm to a new baby? It's horrifying.

What's even more horrifying to me is I had this thought not so long ago—and this is a diary, so I'm allowed to write this down, right?—I had this thought not so long ago that if the governments that approved the mass spraying of chemicals really did wipe out most of Latin America, then I hope that the sad moms with their broken hearts are now at peace. It's my prayer that they and their precious babies are whole and perfect and at peace in Heaven already.

While those of us who lived through the sprayings this month are still here dealing with the fallout.

But even Shell and I could see the reaction to mosquitoes was completely screwed up. Out of control. Now? Now I'm living in a retirement center full of mosquito netting waiting for someone to bust in here with a bullhorn and confetti announcing the power grid's been re-established. We have to believe that will happen pretty soon.

But I'm scared about the chances that we're going to have a food supply ever again with the bee populations wiped out. This government went all Age of Ultron on the mosquitoes without thinking about what the overspray might do to other flying insects and, pow, all the pollinators are gone. We learned about that kind of basic stuff my freshman year in biology class. Doesn't it get covered in Bug-Spray-Tech at the County Office on Day 1? It's not like the pockets of humanity that are left out there are planting almond trees and rice paddies for the whole globe. They have their own cliques to feed.

Day Three of Chronicling Post-Apocalyptic Mayhem
September 28th

While I was feeding the parakeets around the center yesterday, I thought about their seeds. (Yes, the center has parakeets in cages to keep the residents entertained, but they're not in the ICU section. That section is amazingly clean and locked down all.the.time.) Anyway, I read the package to see what kind of seeds the birds eat, and it's a pretty varied diet. So I soaked a handful of their food in water overnight—which was no easy thing, let me say. Try getting more than your ration of water away from the kitchen of this place. I certainly couldn't tell anyone I was leaving a container of water sitting around anywhere. Good ol' Bill would accuse me of attracting mosquitoes and set up more of those stinky citronella candles around my room.

Make a note of this, Archeologists of the Future: Nothing bad happened overnight because I had an open container of water in my room.

I rinsed the seeds off this morning and have them sheltered, but still wet, in my room. I'm going to see if I can sprout them. For planting.

I'm sure there are still farmers out there somewhere who know how to do this far better than I do. Here in the center, I think Miss Baurer in Room 7 could give me some tips. Her family had a farm when she was younger. I don't know all the details, but they lost the farm in the '80s. They moved to a place where she and her husband could still have a garden and a couple of chickens. I've heard her tell the stories about it when I've come to the center to do homework.

From what I understand, she couldn't make any real money off the chickens at that point, but she made awesome quiche with their eggs. Apparently, the trick is to fluff the eggs with a little cream—just a little—before you add anything else to the mix. I'll have to get her to teach me this if we're going to survive on chicken eggs in the future.

And then we'll need a goat or a cow for cream.

I bet we could set up an area for chickens here in the center—like in the park out front or in the courtyard—if we could find some and bring them in. (We'll have to tie Bill up somewhere to keep him from flipping out and killing them and burying them to prevent the spread of whatever disease he imagines they'll carry.) It's going to be important to have a food source when we finish raiding the nearby grocery shelves. I've watched those post-apocalyptic shows with the empty, broken store shelves and some lonely zombified clerk lurking near the spoiled meat section.

Now it's happened.

Minus the zombie.

Well. Sort of minus the zombie.

I'm not sure if the sick people out there should be considered zombies or not. They don't know they're sick, so they're zombie-like in that manner. But they're not actively seeking to gnaw the brains of other humans. That's a checkmark in the "Still A Human" column in my mind.

What makes the sick people so dangerous is they're looking for a place to go, a community to join, yet you can't always tell that they're sick. If they have PyreDees, it's going to be obvious within a day or two of contracting it. No hiding that kind of red skin and raging fever. But if they have Zika virus in their blood, they could be sick for the whole week of symptoms, and their symptoms look totally harmless. And depending on which version of Zika it is, they ARE totally harmless to a healthy, non-pregnant person. It's such a difficult thing to determine.

For example, show me one human being in this situation right now who doesn't have blood-shot eyes. We're all walking around with minimal sleep and maximum stress. So the symptom of conjunctivitis shows up in all of us— sick or not.

And headache? I have a headache right now from the stress of moving to a retirement home last week and losing track of my best friend. I have NO CLUE where Shell is right now. We lost the Internet, cell towers, and basic communication with the outside world within a few hours of getting here.

I don't have the joint pain or muscle pain, but those are all symptoms you'd have to ask a person about. You're not going to "see" a headache in a guy who's walked up to the front door of the center asking for a place to spend the night. Unless he's got one of those migraines my mom gets sometimes. That kind of headache you can see.

The few folks that have come up to the front doors during the past week haven't shown big outward signs of headache, okay? But Bill Stevens and Mom have been firm in telling them, "We can't let you in with our elderly population." To be honest, I don't think Bill would let them in because he fears for himself. And Mom fears for me.

The rash? Most people are wearing long sleeves, even in the heat of late September in Southwest Florida, because every news outlet before the outbreak was showing Governor Scott repeating the mantra to wear long sleeves and long pants when outdoors to prevent mosquito bites, which means you won't see a rash on the person unless you're pretty close and pretty intimate with the person. Then, it's too late for you.

Transmission.

I guess my point is what the CDC director was saying before the big outbreak. Tom Frieden was on every news channel saying, "For this reason, many people might not realize they have been infected." What struck me about his interview on one show was he saying, "Symptoms of Zika are similar to other viruses spread through mosquito bites, like Dengue and Chikungunya." I remember telling Mom that I always heard dengue fever was horrible, and I'd never heard of Chikungunya. She told me to research it.

Because that's a total Mom kind of response.

Back then, pre-end-of-the-world, I had access to the Internet, which I miss SO much, and I looked up this stuff. Either the CDC wanted to downplay the horror—a lot—or the invasion of mosquito-bitten travelers with these diseases went ignored when it should have been shouted from the rooftops.

I found out most of the states in the United States had cases of Chikungunya in 2014 and again in 2015. *Most* of them. It was a map of mostly light blue states with a couple not infected. How was this not significant enough to report?

When I had gotten riled up about it, I had told Shell, when things go bad, we'll go to a really cold region like Minnesota to winter it out. Mosquito eggs can't survive a winter there.

Speaking/writing of surviving, I get that people around here are stressed out, but they don't have to be rude. We really need to show each other some compassion. Some of the residents in the center are having a tough time with the changes. It's hardly fair to take out our angst on them. I find myself wishing in one minute that Mom would put the rude people, namely Bill Stevens, in their places, and wishing in the next minute that Mom would send him to a time-out so he can think about the things he's said.

She used to do that to me. She'd send me to sit on this hard bench in the corner of the dining room where I'd have to think about what I'd done or what I'd said. I think I spent half my childhood on that bench. Then! Then I'd have to either apologize for what I'd done or defend what I'd done. Ugh. I got pretty good at hiding the stupid things I did for a while. Or so I thought.

Moms can be sneaky when it comes to finding stuff out. I think she had operatives at my school that reported back to her about things I did—or even wanted to do.

There was this one time when Shell and I were in seventh grade and we wanted to hang out with the cool kids. We had a time and everything set up to go to the gas station at the far side of my subdivision after school to get sodas. One of the kids had a fake I.D. and could buy cigarettes, so some of them were going to smoke. I have never had any desire to smoke because it smells so gross, but Shell said we'd look cool just hanging with them while they did it. I agreed at the time because I was young and stupid.

Somehow, my mom found out about the date beforehand. I still don't know how, but I think she must have been following Shell's Facebook page. I didn't have any mention of it on mine, that's for sure.

Mom got a parent hall pass from the principal and met me at the door of my seventh hour classroom right before school was let out. She took my phone and texted Shell to meet us at our car in the parents' parking lot. Then she drove Shell to her house, told Mrs. Dexter what we had planned to do, and drove me home to that bench in the dining room.

I was embarrassed and mad when I saw her at the classroom door. I didn't believe the things she told us in the car—things about how some cool kids will be mean to younger kids that they suddenly invite into their group—things about bullies who force newbies to drink alcohol until they're sick—things about some cool kids who put younger kids in dangerous situations just because they think it's funny. How they post bad pictures of them all over Snapchat and Instagram to ruin their reputations and chances to get into a good college.

She didn't make me sit on the bench very long that afternoon. She said, "You probably feel sorry for yourself, don't you?" I don't remember exactly how I answered her, but I *was* feeling sorry for myself at the time. "You and Rachelle are beautiful young ladies with strong minds and good character. Please don't let ugly people with weak minds and bad character do harm to you."

Day Four of Chronicling Paranoia
September 29th

Mom gave me a facemask today and told me she doesn't want to see me without it. One might think she's getting paranoid. It's the most annoying thing ever. It's just a formed paper—thick paper—mask that cups your nose and mouth, but it's a sort of one-size-fits-all contraption so it's big enough to swallow half my face. Considering I wear glasses, it rests on my nose under the bridge of the frames, which causes my breath to go up and fog my lenses. Like I said, it's annoying. When she's not in our room, I take it off.

I've been thinking about the way the local governments killed off the mosquitoes—or at least tried to—and the better ways they could have done it. Like bats. If I had a Tablet and access to the Internet, I could look up how many mosquitoes a single bat eats in a year, but I remember it's a lot. In the neighborhood of *thousands* per night. We need to build bat houses and place them around the outside of the center. This will attract bats, which will eat the insects. When Mom comes back to the room, I'll put on my facemask, and tell her this idea.

Now, if I have thought of this, surely other people, older and wiser than I am, have thought of this in other places where people are holed up waiting for help. If other people are building bat houses, maybe we can make a dent in the mosquito population. Of course, that's a little silly now that I re-read it. How many humans are left at this point? How many bat houses can we construct in the far-flung places?

It makes me wonder if there's any hope.

But even if there's small hope, it's still hope.

Day Five of Writing About the Situation
September 30th

Mr. Newson passed away in his sleep this morning. He was the resident in Room 12. I don't know much about him, but his daughter, Marissa Newson, is in her late fifties, and came to stay with him after the first outbreak of PyreDees in early September. Back when only the "crazy" conspiracy theorists were linking the plague with the spraying after Hurricane Hermine.

Miss Newson's been here the whole time, helping the staff and taking care of her dad. I don't think I really paid much attention to her until this morning. I didn't notice how lovely her eyes are. She has the crinkles and wrinkles that older people have, but they're etched like a piece of art, like a malleable statue. The wrinkles around her eyes are deeper today. I wonder if I'm sad because her grief is right there where we can all see it, or if I understand what it's like to lose a dad.

Mr. Newson worked as a roofer for a construction company when he was younger. The skin on his arms looked leathery brown from being sunburned most of his life. Mom said he had survived stage two melanoma cancer a few years ago. She said it like she was proud of him.

Mrs. Jones from Room 2 is going to play the piano while we have a wake for him tonight. I overheard one of the staff—Bill Stevens of course—say he wants to burn the body in the courtyard to repel mosquitoes. That's when I walked back to my room to write this down. I hope Miss Newson didn't hear Bill's comment. I hope none of the residents who are mere days or weeks from death heard it. I hope they don't burn me when I die. But if they do, I hope they don't use those flipping citronella candles in the fire.

Day Six of Writing Down the Happenings
October 1st

A stranger came to the center this morning. She wore a Hazmat suit and carried a metal briefcase. Mom wore her facemask to meet her in the park out front, where they talked for what seemed like forever. In reality, it was half an hour. But when you're watching from a window and can't hear what's going on, it feels like eternity. The hymn "They Come, God's Messengers of Love" kept going through my head while they were talking.

They come to watch around us here
To soothe our sorrow, calm our fear:
But chiefly, at our journey's end
'Tis theirs the spirit to defend.

I know how silly it is, but I was hoping she would have news about Shell and her mom. I know, I know—why would a total stranger know about a specific person who just happens to be connected to someone at this center? But it happens in the movies.

When Mom came back in, she told us the woman's name is Dr. Sheila Frank and she's going to the CDC in Atlanta with vials of mosquito eggs, larvae, pupae, and adults that have been treated and killed with pure Pyrethrum. "It's the essential oil out of the chrysanthemum," Mom said to us. "Apparently, it's not harmful to humans."

Where have I heard that before? On national news, perhaps?

I remember one of the news talk shows had three men on that talked about the "harmful to humans" concept. One was an insect-control guy from a parish in Louisiana. I don't remember too much about him. I think he was trying to convince everyone the conspiracy theorists that didn't trust the aerial spraying were all crazy, and he was petitioning the government to have a coordinated spraying all across the nation. "The biggest IMM in history," he said a lot. IMM meant Integrated Mosquito Management.

One of the guests was a guy who had created a biodegradable solution out of chrysanthemum oils.

Then one was a guy who made miniature robotic insects, which seemed a little sci-fi to me at the time.

I was doing homework, so I wasn't tuned in very well except to hear "the biggest IMM in history" over and over again.

The three argued and yelled over one another so that you could hardly hear or understand what they were saying. The show's host—and I think it was probably Bill O'Reilly because Mom liked to hear what his guests had to say about stuff when he wasn't yelling at them—couldn't keep them under control.

What I remember most about the interview, aside from three grown men turning red in the face as they yelled at each other like children on national television, is the guy with the flower power. At one point, he got quiet while the others—including the host—were yelling. He hung his head down a bit. I thought he was crying. Actual tears. It looked like his chin did that trembling thing that little kids do when they're trying not to break down in front of their parents.

The others did shut up, and the host asked him, "Do you have a final thought for us, Mr. Jensin?" He looked directly in the camera with his eyes kind of glassy from tears and said, "This solution is like everything else we've discussed. It's safe to humans until the government gets hold of it."

Remembering his words, I wondered if Dr. Frank in the Hazmat suit should take her vials of Pyrethrum oil to the CDC or not.

Then Mom said the words that will change the dynamic in this center forever. "She wants to know if anyone from this community wishes to go with her."

Of course Bill Stevens jumped at that. Even though he's only been at the center since he graduated back in the spring, he's going to represent his faction of staff this afternoon when he and Mom go out to ask Dr. Frank some more questions. I'm going to take notes…surreptitiously.

Later on Day Six of Things Still Sucking

I have a feeling Mom knows I was eavesdropping this afternoon. She's been doing that "Momming" thing this evening. You know…when they offer you comfort food and smile in that "I love you so much" sort of way while you eat it. I think she's trying not to ask what I heard. It's like she doesn't know how to fix it. And I want to tell her it's okay. So we ate tomato bisque and smiled at each other in a sort of soup-and-smile dance of our spoons.

I'll tell you what I heard. I took a screenwriting course in a summer school creative writing track and haven't had a chance to put the skills to use, so I'll write it out like a screenplay. First, I set the scene.

FADE IN:

EXT. CENTER'S PARK — DAY

Mom, Bill and Dr. Sheila Frank are seated on stone benches that face one another in a circle around some flowers and a birdbath that has been turned upside-down for weeks. None of them notice the teen taking notes in a spiral notebook behind the shrubbery between them and the Naples Cares life plan community building.

Dr. Frank is still in her Hazmat suit except for the helmet, which she has set beside her on the metal briefcase on the bench.

                    MOM
Can I offer you some water?

                 DR. SHEILA FRANK
Thank you.

MOM

This is Nursing Technician Bill Stevens. He's been with Naples Cares since graduation, and was one of our interns before that. Bill, this is Doctor Sheila Frank from NCH.

DR. SHEILA FRANK

Good to meet you, Bill. You'll forgive me if I don't shake hands.

BILL

Of course. Don't want to get too close.

MOM

Bill is interested in hearing more about your journey to Atlanta.

DOCTOR SHEILA FRANK
(laughs lightly)

Journey. How apropos. What used to be less than a two-hour flight from R.S.W. is now...I don't even know...depending on how clogged Seventy-Five will be...at least a solid two days of driving time...but stopping to find gas? I have no idea how difficult or easy this *journey* as you call it will be once I get to the interstate.

BILL

Do you think you'll have much trouble on the interstate?

DOCTOR SHEILA FRANK

Very much so. People reacted to the outbreak of PyreDees as if it were something they could get away from, and they fled the cities for rural areas. Unfortunately, when their cars ran out of gas in the bumper-to-bumper traffic, some people just got out and left them. It'll take some fancy driving to get over the bridges and around Sarasota, Tampa, Gainesville, and so on.

BILL
(nods)

DOCTOR SHEILA FRANK
I anticipate I'll need to leave my vehicles at some of the bridges.

MOM
Are you basing this on actual recon?

DOCTOR SHEILA FRANK
(smiles)
It's not all from Hollywood, my friend. I had a lab assistant who is responsible for much of the work in extracting the oil from the chrysanthemums, and he made it to I-Seventy-Five and back to the lab at the hospital in about an hour—on a bicycle, not in a car—and reported what he saw.

(She pauses and looks to the sky.)
It's not pretty out there.

(She looks back to her audience.)
A lot of people gave up without a fight. It's as if the PyreDees was more than they wanted to deal with. As if they just no longer cared to try. They sat down and died of the disease. He said there are people sitting in their cars...just dead. The stench is unbearable as you near a congested area. The buzzing of flies is almost deafening.

BILL
(interrupting her)
Wait. There are people who left their cars and people who died in their cars?

DOCTOR SHEILA FRANK
Yes. Both. My working hypothesis is that we have two factions of humans. We have the healthy people like the three of us who did not get hit with the sprays.

Then we have people infected with one of the Zika strains, and who had the wherewithal to either hunker down and wait it all out or get out of the cities and keep going. An unfortunate majority of those who fled were infected with PyreDees and had no chance to recover. If they were in the process of escaping the cities, they would have died wherever they lost the will to live. Anyone caught outside during the aerial spraying is going to end up with PyreDees, as you know.

BILL
So you're saying the mosquitoes aren't dangerous?

DOCTOR SHEILA FRANK
(sighs)
I'm not sure of that. I don't believe that a healthy human adult is in extreme danger from the original mosquitoes. The *Aedes aegypti* and *Aedes albopictus*. But the genetically modified insects that were released to attack the *Aedes* subspecies have agents in addition to the ADA in their saliva that corrupted the Zika virus. I think those mosquitoes are remarkably dangerous to everyone.

MOM
My daughter has an idea for us in this new era. She remembers how to build bat houses, and suggested we put

some up around compounds where people live. Natural mosquito control.

BILL
(snorts with derision to totally dismiss my idea)

DOCTOR SHEILA FRANK
That's a great idea. It's obviously not going to eradicate the mosquito population overall, but it will certainly protect people in localized areas if it brings the bats in. As I travel north, I'll spread that idea.

MOM
I'll let her know. You mentioned the modified mosquitoes' saliva and ADA. I don't think I remember what ADA is?

DOCTOR SHEILA FRANK
It's adenosine deaminase, which is a protein. When the mosquito bites, it injects saliva with proteins that anesthetize the bitten area. The genetically modified mosquitoes have an additional protein in their saliva. My assistant was close to isolating the extra protein when…when he succumbed to PyreDees.

MOM
I'm so sorry.

DOCTOR SHEILA FRANK
Thank you. It was a difficult experience. I sincerely hope you don't have to see it happen to anyone you care about.

BILL

How far along was he with the work? Do you have any of his research with you? Maybe I can continue?

DOCTOR SHEILA FRANK

He accidentally destroyed a table of specimens and notes. I tried to piece together some of his research, but I'm afraid we'll need to gather new adults and pupae.

BILL
(frowning)

Accidentally destroyed a table? How does a professional accidentally destroy—

MOM
(interrupts him tersely)

Bill.

DOCTOR SHEILA FRANK

At some point near the end of the disease, the infected person gives up, you see. He or she will just lie down. In my son's case, he closed his eyes and fell. He was still breathing. I could feel his pulse through the gloves of my suit, but he had worked right up until he lost the will to even open his eyes.

MOM
(turns away and wipes tears from her eyes)
DISSOLVE:

Day Seven of Recording the Stress
October 2nd

We had a worship service because it's Sunday, and Eunice Jones in Room 2 can play the piano beautifully to lead us in singing hymns. It was especially important because Bill Stevens took three of the staff to go with Dr. Sheila Frank this morning, which is a hardship for those of us remaining with the residents. I can help out a bit, and Marissa Newson has stayed to help out, but we'll miss having four qualified nurses working with elderly patients who have different medical needs.

Even though we need to ration food, and we know this is going to be tough without them here, we had a big breakfast to send them on their way. Mom surprises me. Even though Bill has been nothing but a pain in the neck the whole time he's worked here, Mom hugged him before he left and told him to be careful. She prayed over him and gave him some books of matches that I know she had stashed in her bug-out bag. He'll need those to burn the obnoxious citronella candles that none of us can get away from.

Yes, Mom has a bug-out bag.

My mom isn't exactly what you'd call a "prepper". She wouldn't have been a candidate for one of the documentaries on the Discovery Channel where the people talk about an old box car they've bought and buried with a secret trap door that leads down to it—and to a stockpile of canned goods and hydroponic plants with grow-lights.

But she does have a bug-out bag for herself, one for me and one for Shell in the event Shell is at our house when we have to run for the hills.

My bag contains food like granola bars and Vienna sausages, a couple LifeStraw filters, books of matches in a few snack-size baggies, glow sticks, a bizarre metallic-looking blanket-in-an-envelope, binoculars with night vision, a change of clothes squished into a gallon-size Ziploc bag, a flare gun, a pack of sanitizing wipes, a Swiss

Army knife, rope, actual bullets for the pistol Mom has in her bag, and general stuff to keep us alive if we get stuck out on the road somewhere.

What makes it truly a work of art is the layering.

The bag is a huge backpack. A huge backpack that weighs more than I like to carry. But Mom made it in layers.

It has a stainless steel frame with an actual tent rolled up and attached near the base, sort of at the lower back area. If you have to lose some weight in a hurry, you can pull a cord that releases the tent and lets the weight shift down to the lower back. It also has a matching fanny pack that is attached to the bug-out bag at all times.

Until you're running from something scary.

If you're running from something zombie-like scary and you're losing ground, you can unclasp the fanny pack, which remains belted to your body, and drop the heavy bug-out bag. The fanny pack doesn't have as many goodies in it, of course, but it'll keep you alive until you can get to some kind of shelter.

Or so Mom has told me.

I have to think that sitting in this room writing in this diary isn't going to keep me alive. Not much cardio training in writing on paper. I need to get back into the habit of exercising the way I had to do for gym class. If I need to carry that bug-out bag anywhere, I'll need the stamina.

My P.E. teacher would pass out if he read that paragraph. Remember: I'm a nerd who enjoys the books and old-time music. I'm better at fixing the radio Mike has in the boiler room than lifting Miss Turner in Room 3 to a sitting position. Physical Education and games of sport are not my forte. But Mr. Carter could get me to run a lap or two if he threatened my G.P.A.

Thinking about Mr. Carter, I have to wonder how many of my teachers have made it this far. There were a couple teachers this year who seemed like they could stand up to any virus you threw at them. Strong men and women who could kick anything in the teeth, you know? It's sad to think they might not be alive any longer.

It makes me think of Shell and her mom. Where did they go after that last text I sent? Why weren't they at their house when we drove by to get them? Why didn't Shell tell me where they were going?

Day Eight of Writing it Down
October 3rd

Let me be a total nerd and start with this:

Dear Diary, I have such exciting news to share today!
Shell is here!

I was too excited to write it last night, but while I was writing yesterday, it was as if Rachelle Dexter knew I was writing about her, as if she knew I was trying to reach out in the universe and find her, my BF since first grade, my partner in so many crimes, my soul sister and confidante, the one who keeps me from losing my mind when the Internet is down...she's here!

I was too surprised to believe it when I first saw her walking through the park in front of the center with some kind of plastic crate slung over her shoulder and leaking straw. She was probably ten or twelve steps from the place where Mom and Bill had been talking with Dr. Frank before I realized, yes, it really was Shell and not my brain just imagining that my bestie had lived through the past two weeks of insanity and death and chaos and crap. I saw her crazy red curly hair all mussed up as if she hadn't washed or brushed it in the whole two weeks since I'd seen her last and it reminded me of the dear Helen Burns in *Jane Eyre*.

My best friend *ever* is here!

Here's what happened. Some of it is sad, so brace yourself.

On the night that things started to really break down along the East Coast of the United States, the 21st of September, Governor Scott called on everyone to be in their homes for a 7 p.m. Eastern/6 p.m. Central curfew. A huge aerial spraying of IMM would take place from 7:30-9:30 p.m. Eastern/6:30-8:30 p.m. Central. This was a statewide spraying to eradicate the *Aedes aegypti* and *Aedes albopictus* in all stages of growth, including eggs. Planes were taking off from a number of airfields to cover the state. This was happening all over the United States and in Canada, Mexico, Puerto Rico, The Caribbean and all across South America. A coordinated assault on the insects that were killing our babies and elderly on the U.N. International Day of Peace.

I remember Mom barreling into the living room where I watched the press conference with my piles of books and homework. She carried the battery charger with its green light boldly shining at me like a Cyclops. She pointed at my cell phone on the couch next to me and told me to call Shell. Not text her. Call her. Tell her to get her mom and a change of clothes and be at their front door in ten minutes. "And get your bug-out bags!" she had called to me as she flew to the kitchen.

Mom doesn't have that crazy parental tone of obey-me-now very often, so when she uses it, I don't hesitate. I didn't have time to tell her Shell had skipped school that day. I just had to obey.

I also had to leave Shell a voice mail while I was pulling my bag and hers out from under my bed and flopping them on top of my bed. I stopped to text her the message, too, while Mom came into my room and literally sprayed me down with bug spray. It was disgusting. The smell. OMG. But she was in that funky parental mode that I wasn't going to interrupt.

"Did Shell answer?" she asked me. I told her no, but that I'd just texted her, and she said that was good. We were stopping by there to grab them. I remember asking where we were going, but Mom was already moving again. I scooped one bag onto each shoulder, which, let me tell you, is not easy. I had to turn sideways to scoot out my door and sort of side-skip down the hallway, but Mom was moving fast, and I knew she expected me to do the same.

"The trunk's open. Throw those in with the water, Babe."

It was the calmest order she'd given yet, and I took advantage of her having her back to me to grab the fluffy pillow off the couch in my free hand, tuck it under the arm with my cell phone, and grab my history book.

I'm not sure how my brain knew to pack the trunk of the car. I just knew to align the bags next to each other with the pillow on top, in front of the gallons of water Mom had lined in three neat rows at the back, leaving the exact amount of room her bag needed, plus a plastic egg crate of canned food she set down in front of it. She nestled it just right, laid a shotgun across it all with one of those garment bags atop that, and slammed the trunk closed.

I remember her winking at me as she put her hand on my shoulder. "That's my good girl. Whatever you see on the road, stay my strong, wise girl, okay?"

That made sense once we got out of the subdivision and onto Immokalee Road where I think half the state was trying to run each other over. I heard her swear more than once, always under her breath as if I couldn't be subjected to such language. Once she said, "should've bought an SUV." Another time she said, "should've bought a Hummer."

When we got to Shell's house, the lights were out. The lights all up and down the block were out. She ordered me to stay in the car while she ran up to the door. It felt like forever that she stood on the porch before I saw her unlock the door and go in. Another lifetime later she came back out with a notebook of some kind and Shell's smart phone, both of which she put on my lap as she drove across the soggy lawn.

I thought it was nice that she gave me a scrapbook Shell had made of us from when we were kids, running through a sprinkler with the basset hound Trixie, swinging at the neighborhood playground, attending our first concert, acting in our first school play. It must have been out where it caught Mom's eye, because she wouldn't have wasted time looking for such a thing while looking for our friends. I also thought it was nice that she pulled the door closed on her way back out. I had figured out we were in pretty serious trouble and there wasn't a lot of time to mess around, so it was a nice gesture—locking the door as we left.

But the thing that shook me while I sat there, rocking against my seatbelt as she tore through Shell's neighborhood, was the smart phone. "Are they okay?" I asked her as we drove away.

She told me, "I hope so, Sweetie. Their car's not in the garage. Trixie's not in the house. Text Joanna…"

I asked, "Where should they meet us?"

That's why Mom had hesitated. She didn't look at me. And she didn't answer. I guessed we were going to the Naples Cares, so that's what I texted to Mrs. Dexter.

And that's why I spent two weeks glancing out the windows here. I wanted to see Shell and Joanna Dexter drive up the lane to the resident drop-off doors. It filled me with such relief to see my best friend yesterday that I didn't notice for the longest time that she was alone. Her mom wasn't with her.

When Mom and I were stuck on Immokalee Road in traffic, she would look at the car clock, and then do some crazy move around traffic that on any other evening would have gotten us arrested. I remember thinking there were too many people out for them to all get home in time for the curfew. I remember listening to the hymn on the radio and thinking it was a little dark for the night's activities.

An angel guard to us supply,
When on the bed of death we lie;
And by Thine own almighty power,
O shield us in the final hour.

Mom didn't seem to notice when I changed the station to one of the news channels, which wasn't any lighter.

By the time 7 p.m. hit, we were within a few minutes of the center—but only if there were no other crazy drivers between our goal and us. Mom was clearly stressed out. At one point she called the center and asked for Dr. Arlington, the director. He wasn't there. As the next senior staff member, she would be in charge when she arrived, which has been a good thing all along.

So she asked for the janitor. "Mike! Thank God you're there. Please turn off the A.C."

He must have complained because she turned on her mom-being-polite-yet-very-firm voice and said, "Mike, we cannot let the aerial spray get into our residents' lungs tonight. Period. We'll get sued by their families. You must turn off the A.C. and do something to close all vents to the outside. Use only re-circulated and filtered air like the clean room has for I.C. residents."

That worked and Mom finished the call letting him know we'd be there soon and we'd be using the unloading bay on the side of the kitchen. She's good at thinking fast on her feet—or when driving in frustrating traffic. Maybe that's why she's not only a nurse, but also the assistant director of the Naples Cares life plan community.

I don't know how soon after that the cell towers went down, but phone lines were congested that night. Neither of us was able to get a call out to anyone. Our focus was on finding the best way around stalled cars and drivers who weren't willing to break the laws. It took us the whole thirty minutes, but she drove through puddles the size of ponds that other drivers seemed to be avoiding and actually rammed one little Smart Car out of the way in one intersection, and pulled our Oldsmobile right up to the kitchen bay, popping the trunk as she threw it in park.

Mike must have been watching. He opened the door so Mom didn't have to waste time using her key. She put the garment bag over my shoulder and pushed me toward the door, saying to go to the conference room and wait for her there. I knew better than to argue, even though I could have helped get more out of the car. I heard the engine of a plane. I knew one was coming, and its spray would be right behind.

I wasn't even through the kitchen when I heard the trunk slam and the door slam after. The deadbolt clicked and I glanced back to see Mom set the plastic crate of food heavily onto the counter. She and Mike were loaded down with the crate, pillow, gun and three bug-out bags. There was no way they could get all the water jugs in. But at least they were in and the poison was not.

That was a difficult night to get through. It didn't take long for the center to get warm, and warmer, and warmer. The residents started to complain about the stuffiness and stillness. Mom offered them pleasant excuses when the more aware folks asked about back-up generators and recycled air. I remember thinking the smell of bug spray would never get out of the fancy conference room chair I fell asleep in.

Shell and her mom had it worse. They had tried to go to Mrs. Dexter's mother's house in Tallahassee. Of course, Tallahassee had gotten the brunt of Hurricane Hermine at the beginning of September, and people were still recovering from the flooding left behind. The mosquito population soared out of control there. And into Georgia, South Carolina, and all up the East Coast where the storm surge had caused flooding and impossible standing water conditions.

All up and down I-10 and I-75 where Mrs. Dexter needed to drive, from Leon to Hillsborough counties, older houses manufactured in the 1990s and earlier were missing sections of roof and panes of glass where either category-one hurricane or tropical storm force winds had ripped and torn and flung everything from tree limbs to decorative planters into homes. They had gotten as far as Tampa before they learned that Mrs. Schild—Shell's grandma—had succumbed to the symptoms of Zika.

Shell said her mom didn't know what to do. Mrs. Dexter had thought about calling my mom, but her cell had run out of juice and they realized they'd left Shell's at home. They tried to Skype on Shell's Tablet, but everything was slow and cell towers were jammed with people trying to do the same thing they were trying. People in more than Gulf Coast cities of Florida.

They sat at a Flying-J outside of Tampa for the night of the curfew before Mrs. Dexter decided they should go back home. Shell was exhausted from all the stress, and curled up to sleep with Trixie in one of the lockable restroom stalls.

The interstate was a mess the next morning, of course. Shell said they ran out of gas on an off-ramp near Sarasota. They hitched a ride with a trucker taking pallets of hens to slaughter. Shell was horrified by the thought, but, really, what other way could they be transported that would have been any more comfortable? Each pallet held crate upon crate of individually caged hen on a bed of straw. Clucking in confusion.

When the truck reached its inevitable end, and the trucker lost contact with one driver after another, he handed Shell and Mrs. Dexter a pair of chickens each and wished them well. He started walking north. They never saw him again. Shell opened all the crates and let all the chickens roam where they would. Her two hens she stuffed into one crate together, threw in some of their feed, rigged one of the ties that had held the pallets down into a makeshift harness so she could carry the crate on her back, and led her mom south toward Naples. She had no reason to believe Mrs. Dexter was sick at that point. As they walked south, they passed cars without travelers, of course, but as nightfall approached, they came upon some that had people just sitting in them, sweltering in the heat.

Mrs. Dexter cautioned Shell not to bother the people, not to go near them for fear that they'd be dangerous thugs or kidnappers. To Shell, it seemed natural that her argument against being kidnapped amid the lines of motionless cars worked. Her mom eventually shrugged and let Shell talk to one of the families sitting on the side of the highway.

The small group sat on their luggage, staring into the nothingness of quietly approaching dusk. One of the children closed her eyes when Trixie barked at them and while Shell asked if they wanted to walk with her and her mom to Naples. The father blinked and shook his head. She remembered he sounded very tired as he said, "there's no point."

He appeared flushed with fever, so she didn't get too close to him. Mrs. Dexter had cried when they walked away from the family, but Shell needed to get distance between them. She felt something bad happening on the highway.

Of course she had no way of knowing that all those people were the latest victims of the PyreDees plague, but she'd seen enough scary movies to know she had to get to shelter before nightfall when monsters started coming out of the shadows.

The Waffle House she led her mom to was nearly vacant, its lights running off a generator that she said sputtered behind the building like it was about to run dry. Three people sat at one corner table, seeming to watch nothing. Trixie barked at them, but none of them seemed to care that Shell brought a basset hound into the restaurant.

Shell told me it was as if no one even heard her deep, hound-dog voice echo off the almost empty restaurant walls. Not one of them complained about the two chickens in the crate Shell set on the floor next to a table where she helped her mom take a seat. She put Trixie's leash in her mom's hand, as if her mom were going to do anything to stop the dog from running across the restaurant if the hound decided to go after the three patrons, and went to find something for them to drink.

Mrs. Dexter wouldn't eat or drink anything that Shell offered her. Shell ate bread smeared with grape jelly from the packets in the black plastic bowl at the table and drank room-temperature bottled water. She filled her pockets with the jelly packets and put water in the bowl for Trixie, who acted thrilled to drink. The hens were happy to drink and eat bread, too. The three patrons in the corner wanted nothing that Shell offered them. And still Mrs. Dexter wanted nothing. At one point, her mom told her she should lock the front doors so no one else could get in. It was the last thing Mrs. Dexter said that made sense.

At least, while Shell told the story, it was the last thing she was willing to share with me. Shell's red, tired eyes filled with tears as she spoke her mother's words.

From my side of the window outside the intensive care unit, I put my hand on the cool glass as if I could touch my friend. I wanted to give her comfort. I told her she didn't have to try to remember everything at once. There'd be time to talk after she'd had some rest. From what she said, she'd been walking for eleven days to reach us. She agreed with that, and then said, "no…I rode a bicycle for a while. After Trixie…"

I didn't ask her to elaborate. I didn't want to know that poor Trixie had succumbed to the same disease the humans had contracted. It wasn't fair and I didn't want to hear about it. But she looked at me with her sad eyes and said, "I think Trixie was too old to get any of those viruses."

I only nodded, not trusting my voice. I wanted to hug her and tell her she was safe now, but Mom had told me not to go into the IC room with her. I understood that. We needed to make sure Shell was healthy after her ordeal before we had her out among the elderly residents of the center.

After removing her gloves and mask, Mom came out of the ICU with one of those "I love you so much" smiles for me. "You need to get your rest."

I had questions for her, of course. Shell was exhausted from her ordeal and obviously ready to sleep for days. I wanted to know what medicine Mom had given her. It made perfect sense that she'd given her something for her headache and plenty of fluids by I.V. Poor Shell was so dehydrated that she couldn't really stand taking in a lot of water or soup or anything. As Mom led me back to our room, I asked her if we had anything we could give Shell to soothe her sunburn. Now it's morning and I have asked Tameka, the remaining nurse, to find something with Aloe Vera in it.

I've written a lot this morning while watching Mom change the saline bags for Shell and try to give her juice. It's made me tired, worrying so much and writing so much. I'm really glad to have my friend here now.

Day Nine of Continuing On and On
October 4th

I think Shell is really sick. I pray it's not the PyreDees, but Mom won't give me a straight answer. The two chickens she brought with her died some time in the night, so my plan to repopulate the earth with Chic-fil-A has had a setback. We're afraid to eat them because we don't know what they died of or if their meat is tainted.

Ann Parker in Room 1 and Tom Stewart in Room 11 both passed away in the night.

A man from the news station came to the front doors mid-morning. We couldn't let him in, of course, but he told us the power grid is supposed to come back online any day now all across the Southeast. He said Washington D.C. and one of the major cities in Mexico—I forget which one he named—already has power.

Isn't that a strange way to get news in the year 2016? The reporter comes to your front door. He must not be as tired as the rest of us are. He left some citronella candles in a box outside the door for us. We told him of the idea to construct bat houses in areas where there are groups of humans to protect from mosquitoes and he's going to share that everywhere he goes.

Day Ten
October 5th

Placebo effect. It's a placebo effect when you tell someone you've given them a medicine that's helping them, but you've really just given them a sugar pill or something like that. Like burning those horrid citronella candles to keep mosquitoes away. I don't think those candles work as well as letting bats come and eat the mosquitoes. But all day yesterday and today, Mom has told me that she's used the backup generator to turn the A.C. back on and that we have cool air here in the center. She's telling me this to make me feel better about being trapped in this sweltering and humid building, and I appreciate that, but it's not working. I know she's telling me stories the way she told the residents pleasant little stories the first night we were here—the night of the coordinated spraying. The IMM. Because I know it's just recycled, warm air from a backup generator, I'm not feeling any cooler. But I don't want to complain. I know she has other things to deal with. Poor Shell is very sick, and Mom is working with Tameka—the only nurse who stayed—to get her well. Then Melissa Turner in Room 3 died yesterday and her sister, Melody Turner in Room 4, died last night. It's as if all the residents are giving up, which is such a shame. This crisis is almost over. The news reporter said so. The people who had PyreDees have died off and the rains all over the country have been washing things down. We'll all be able to go back to our homes soon.

Day 11

Patrice Jackson in Room 8 died, but I don't remember when.
Mom seems more affected by today's news than any other.

Twelth Day

I have trouble writing today.
I'm sick of citronella.

Afterword
By Dr. Sheila Frank

At the re-opening of the Naples Cares life plan community February 25, 2018, I was honored to witness Dr. Martin Arlington dedicate the refurbished building to Nursing Technician Bill Stevens who accompanied me to the Centers for Disease Control and Prevention during the difficult and frightening time in September of 2016. Bill will be receiving his advanced degree this spring and will accept the position of Assistant Director at the center, which is obviously going to be just a stepping-stone in his career.

What's most interesting about this day is not the resurrection of a medical care center that many had believed should be burned down due to contagion, but that at the end of the ceremony, a lovely college student with flaming red hair came up to me and handed me a green spiral notebook. She looked at me with solemn eyes and told me, "It's always the survivors who write the history books. I hope you'll make an exception for a friend of mine."

She disappeared into the crowd of people while I thumbed through some of the pages, but I now have the distinct impression that she provided documentation of the center's tribulation that should have been shared before now. As I looked across the courtyard with its decorative bat houses and meticulously groomed chrysanthemum beds, I wondered how much of the center's success is owed to people the current residents will never meet.

THE END